to mom & dad

Published by Peter Pauper Press, Inc.
202 Mamaroneck Avenue
White Plains, New York 10601
U.S.A.

Published in the United Kingdom and Europe by Peter Pauper Press, Inc.
c/o White Pebble International
Unit 2, Plot 11 Terminus Rd.
Chichester, West Sussex PO19 8TX, UK

Library of Congress Cataloging-in-Publication Data

Names: Marcero, Deborah, author, illustrator.
Title: Ursa's light / Deborah Marcero.
Description: First edition. | White Plains, New York : Peter Pauper Press,
    Inc., 2016. | Summary: "One night Ursa the bear had an idea. An amazing
    idea. A wild idea. She was going to fly!"-- Provided by publisher.
Identifiers: LCCN 2015027170 | ISBN 9781441318817 (hardcover : alk. paper)
Subjects: | CYAC: Bears--Fiction. | Flight--Fiction.
Classification: LCC PZ7.1.H47 Ur 2016 | DDC [Fic]--dc23
2015027170

ISBN 978-1-4413-1881-7
Manufactured for Peter Pauper Press, Inc.
Printed in Hong Kong

7 6 5 4 3 2 1

Visit us at www.peterpauper.com

Ursa's Light

Deborah Marcero

Peter Pauper Press, Inc.
White Plains, New York

There were ALL the bears.

And then, there was Ursa.

Ursa liked to imagine anything was possible.

And one night her imagination sparked an idea.

This idea was
a wild thing.

It stirred her
imagination.

It invaded her
dreams . . .

. . . all night long.

When Ursa woke up,
she sprinted around the apartment,
jumped on the furniture,
and reached for the sky.
Then with a booming voice,
Ursa declared . . .

Her parents worried.

Her little brother watched.

Her friends were skeptical.

Still, Ursa believed.
So every day she watched
things in the world that could fly.

"I just know it's possible,"
she would say out loud to anyone,
"and I aim to prove it."

She took notes on the pigeons in the park and designed a kind of flying suit.

But it didn't quite work out.

She noticed that dandelion seeds would lift off
like tiny rockets, so she built her own.

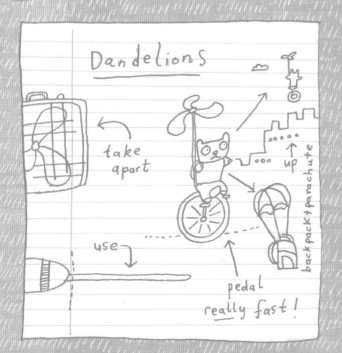

But that didn't quite work either.

She saw that bats would swoop and glide
like graceful shadows.

Nothing seemed to work.

Just when she thought, "Maybe it's true. Maybe I can't . . ." her baby brother pointed toward a big oak tree.

BE A COMET IN

The Cosmos

Needed:
⭐ Shooting Star
10 AM Auditions
TOMORROW

Central Park
Outdoor Theater

Come fly with us!

That night, Ursa could barely sleep.

The next day at the try-out, when her turn came, Ursa remembered all the times she was frustrated and all the times she failed.

AUDITIONS 10 AM

Ursa!

DIRECTOR

Poof!!

She channeled the strength
of the pigeon,

the lightness
of the dandelion seed,

the agility of
the bat,

and a huge internal ROAR . . .

... into the most dynamic shooting star
anyone had ever seen.

Needless to say,
she got the part.

Opening night of *The Cosmos* . . .

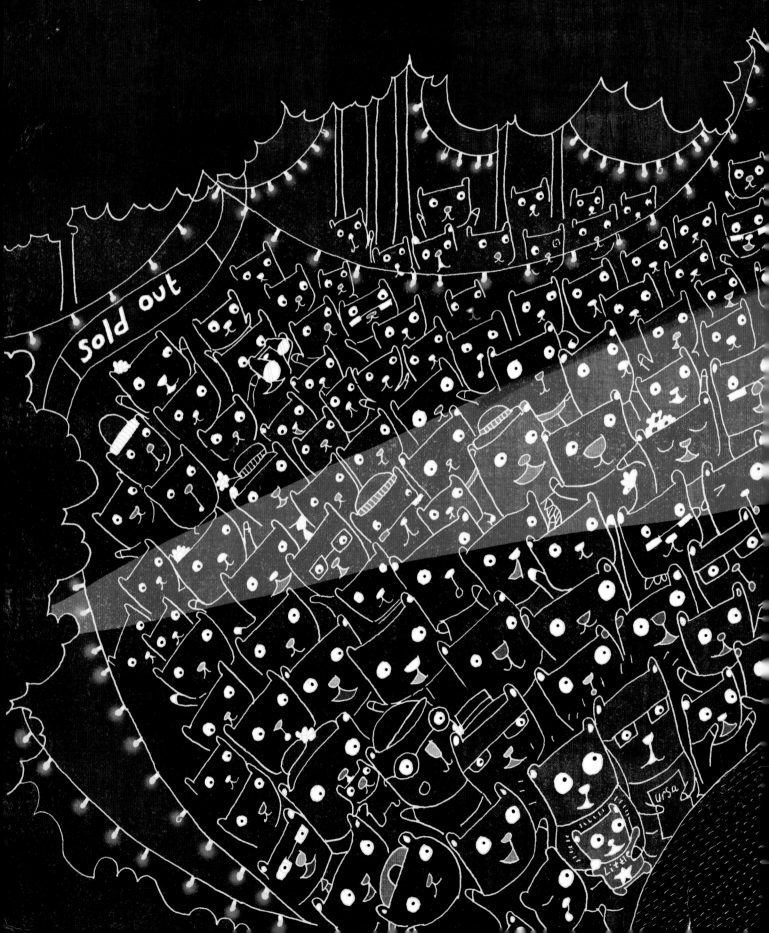

The Cosmos

. . . . her brother glowed.
Her parents beamed.
Her friends cheered.

And Ursa's spirit soared.